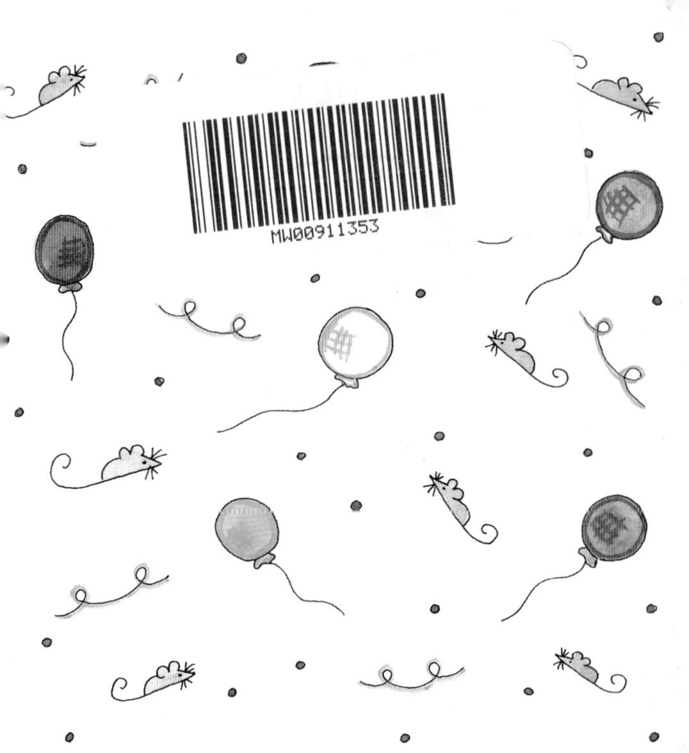
MW00911353

First published in the United States 1994
by Dutton Children's Books,
a division of Penguin Books USA Inc.
375 Hudson Street
New York, New York 10014
Originally published in Great Britain 1994
by Campbell Books
Printed in Singapore
First American Edition
1 3 5 7 9 10 8 6 4 2
ISBN 0-525-45237-0

Mouse Birthday

Michelle Cartlidge

DUTTON CHILDREN'S BOOKS
NEW YORK

It's Mouse's birthday.

Everyone at the party

has brought a present.

This present is from
Mouse's sister.
It is for playtime.

Let's open it.

This present is from
Mouse's brother.
It is for story time.

Let's open it.

This present is from
Mouse's aunt.
It is for teatime.

Let's open it.

This present is from
Mouse's uncle.
It is for busy time.

Let's open it.

This present is from
Mouse's grandmother.
It is for bedtime.

Let's open it.

This present is from
Mouse's grandfather.
It is for springtime.

Let's open it.

This present is from
Mouse's mother and father.
Happy birthday, Mouse!

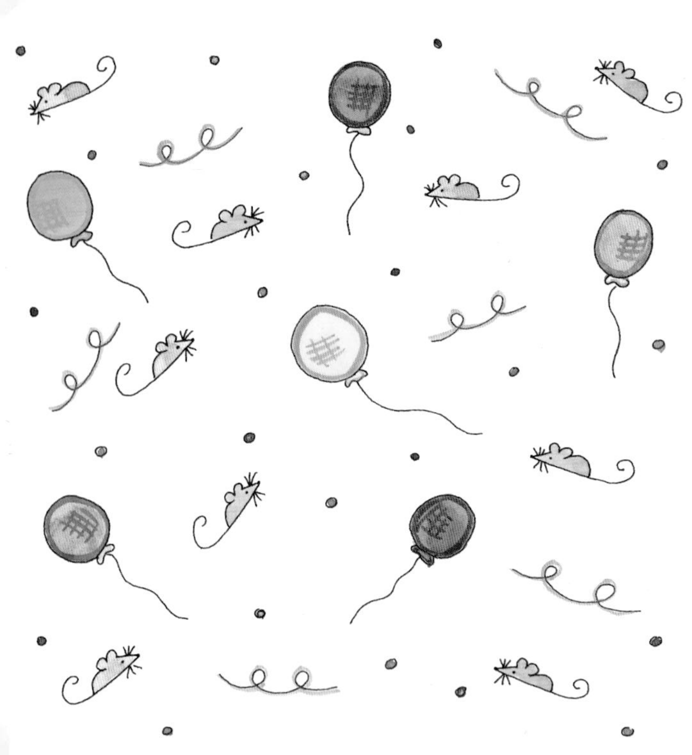